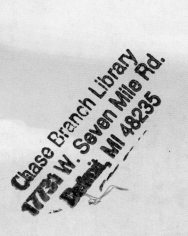

# If You Ever Want to Bring a Piano to the Beach, DON'T!

## Elise Parsley

Little, Brown and Company
New York   Boston

If your mom says to get
ready to play at the beach,
she means with a boat,
or a Frisbee,
or a shovel.

She is **not** talking about the piano.

You'll tell her that it's okay.
You will hold on tight to your piano
and keep it neat and clean,
and you'll even promise
to push it to the beach yourself—
cross your heart.

But on the way, your arms will get heavy.

Then your legs will get draggy.

So you'll find the perfect way
to move the piano along.

When you feel rested,
you will push again.

Once you're
at the beach,
you'll need to make sure
the piano still works.

Finally, you'll stop for a lunch break.

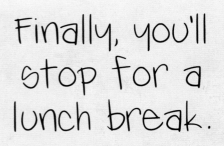

The seagulls will
want to share your
egg-and-cheese sandwich.

This,
you know,
is not good for the piano.

But you'll know just what to do.

Bath time!

You'll splish. You'll splash.
The piano will bob up

and up

and down

and down,

then up
and away...

and out of reach.

By now, of course,
you'll wish you had played
with a boat, or a Frisbee, or a shovel
at the beach instead of the piano.
By now, you'll wish you had
played with your baby sister
instead of the piano.
You'll be so mad, you will want to

# just go home!

Well, here's what
I would do if I were you:

Borrow your brother's fishing line
and cast it far, far out
to catch your drifting piano.

Then, when you reel the line in, you might get your piano back.

Or you might get...

a boat,

or a **Frisbee,**

or a **Shovel.**

Yeah, if you ever want to bring a piano to the beach, don't. You might lose it.

But you never know
what you might find.

For Jarrod, who sometimes loses our nice things

## About This Book

The illustrations for this book were digitally drawn in Adobe Photoshop and then painted in Corel Painter using a Monoprice tablet. This book was edited by Andrea Spooner and designed by Phil Caminiti. The production was supervised by Erika Schwartz, and the production editor was Wendy Dopkin. This book was printed on 128 gsm Gold Sun matte. The text was set in McPea, a custom font made from the artist's handwriting.